Common Senses

by Tom Sullivan

Illustrated by
Rick Reinert

Written by
**Tom Sullivan
and Ron Kidd**

Ideals Publishing Corp.
Milwaukee, Wisconsin

Copyright © MCMLXXXII by Ideals Publishing Corporation,
Tom Sullivan and Rick Reinert
ISBN 0-8249-8022-0

 $\mathcal{H}$ erman Wise-Old-Owl is my name, and seeing is what I do best. In fact, seeing was just about all I did. But some very special friends of mine changed all that. They showed me that being alive is a lot more than just seeing. It's also touching, tasting, hearing, and smelling. They brought me to my senses, you might say—all five senses.

It started with a fellow named Percy Q. Porcupine.
Instead of looking at things the way I do, Percy would
touch them—I mean, really touch them. He didn't know
that everything he touched, he hurt. He only knew that the
other animals seemed to stay away from him and that he
spent most of his time alone.

Percy tried to tell himself that being alone wasn't so bad. After all, he lived in a beautiful library filled with the next best thing to friends—books. Percy could use his books to answer just about any questions the other animals might have. Somehow though, no one ever asked.

One day, Percy glanced out the window of his library
and noticed a very strange thing. Renaldo Raccoon, Rona
Rabbit, Sammy Skunk, Buford Badger—all the animals of
the forest went staggering by, coughing and wheezing.
Curious, Percy followed them. They were all headed for the
same place: my home—the nest of Herman Wise-Old-Owl.

"Herman," moaned one, "my head hurts."

"Herman," croaked another, "my throat's sore."

"Herman," all the animals coughed in unison, "what are we going to do?"

I was trying to think of an answer when I heard an outburst from the group. "Ouch!" someone said. "Eep!" cried someone else. Presently, the cause of all the commotion stepped forward—Percy Q. Porcupine.

"I know the answer," Percy exclaimed. He held up a book he was carrying. It was called *Mother Nature's Herbal Remedies*. "The answer's right in here. It says, 'Cuckoo's Nest Flu—commonly found in the forest. Take special vaccine.'"

"How do we take the vaccine?" someone asked.

"Why," Percy answered, "it is injected with a needle."
Reaching behind him, he plucked a quill from his back.
"We can use this."

Alarmed, the animals broke out in an excited chatter. I
waited until the noise quieted down. Then I said,
"Sometimes good things hurt. Listen to Percy; he has a
point."

And that's how Percy Q. Porcupine became the forest doctor. His quiet library is now a bustling office. His medical books are tattered with use. Now when he touches people, they don't say *ouch*—they say *thank you*.

$\mathcal{I}$n the same way that Percy liked to touch, Renaldo Raccoon liked to taste. He would roam the forest, picking wild leaves and berries which were safe to eat. Then he'd wash everything and taste his treasures. Renaldo never knew what surprises the forest would hold for his taste buds.

One summer day, Renaldo passed beneath my tree with a bunch of chestnuts. "I'm on my way home to make a pie," he called up to me. "Would you like a piece, Herman?"

"I've never tasted chestnut pie," I answered. "I prefer bugs. That's what owls always eat."

Renaldo shook his head in disgust. "That's the trouble with all the animals in this forest. They're afraid to try anything new." As he spoke, a peculiar look crossed his face. "Hm, that gives me an idea. I've got to get going, Herman. See you later."

The next few days the forest buzzed with activity. Under Renaldo's direction, the beavers began putting up a building on the bank of the stream. When the other animals asked what it was, Renaldo just answered, "Be here Tuesday night and you'll see."

Tuesday night everyone in the forest gathered outside
the new building. At six o'clock sharp the front door
opened. Out stepped Renaldo Raccoon. Over the door he
hung a sign that said RENALDO'S TASTE EMPORIUM.
Then he turned to the crowd and said, "Come on in,
everyone. I hope you haven't had dinner yet."

Chattering excitedly, the animals went inside and sat
down. Chipmunks in tuxedoes marched out of the kitchen
and set leafy, green salads in front of everyone. Rona
Rabbit and her bunny friends were quick to start eating.
The rest of the animals just sat there.

Renaldo stepped forward. "The idea behind my new restaurant is to show everybody that eating isn't a dull routine—it's an adventure! So tonight I've prepared a wonderful menu of different things. I'd like all of you to at least try everything."

Bruno Bear tore off the corner of one lettuce leaf and, making a face, placed it in his mouth. After a few moments he mumbled, "Not bad." The other animals followed Bruno's example. Soon all the salad was gone.

The main course was trout. This time it was Rona
Rabbit who wouldn't try it. "Rona," said Renaldo, "Bruno
tried your favorite food, so now it's your turn to try his."

A short time later, Rona ordered a second helping of
trout. "It's a little squishy," she said, "but the flavor's
divine!"

And so it went. Each course was a taste adventure for someone. By the end of the evening, every plate was empty including that of Percy Q. Porcupine.

Percy pushed himself back from the table. "Three cheers for Renaldo's Taste Emporium!" he cried.

The cheers rang out, and in the midst of it all, arms folded proudly, stood Renaldo Raccoon—the animal who brought good taste to the forest.

$\mathcal{P}$ercy liked to touch things. Renaldo liked to taste things. And Rona Rabbit liked to hear things. That would have been fine except she also liked to talk.

This often caused trouble. One time she overheard the squirrels discussing where they had hidden their nuts for the winter. She told the chipmunks. They raided the hiding place. Rona didn't know that she started problems with her big ears.

One morning, Rona Rabbit was visiting her friend Buford Badger. Suddenly her ears perked up. There was a new sound in the air. It was so faint she could barely hear it.

"Buford, what's that sound?" she asked.

"Oh, that's just my false teeth clicking. Pay no attention."

"No, not that. The other sound way off in the distance." She shivered and cocked her ears. As the noise grew louder, it began to sound familiar. It reminded her of the sounds she heard when she walked downstream where the brook flowed into a river. It seemed now like the river was coming closer and . . . .

"It is coming closer!" she exclaimed. "That's the sound of rushing water—a lot of it, and it's coming this way! The beaver dam must have broken. The whole forest is in danger!"

Buford snorted. "Must be your imagination."

"There's no time for arguing, Buford! Go to the top of Forest Hill. I'll send the others up to join you. Hurry!"

Rona set off through the forest, hopping as fast as her powerful legs would carry her. She stopped at every mound and tree and thicket, warning everyone a giant wall of water was coming their way. Even though no one but Rona could hear it yet, she knew that if they waited to find out for themselves, it would be too late.

Two hours later, Rona and her friends stood on high ground looking down at the scene before them. The river had pounded through the forest crushing everything in its way. Now, where homes had stood, there was only rubble.

"What are we going to do?" someone asked.

Percy Q. Porcupine stepped forward. "We're going to rebuild. But first we're going to thank Rona. Because she loves to listen, not a single animal was hurt. We still have each other, and we still have the forest."

The animals looked at their friend Rona Rabbit, then gazed down at their forest home. In the stillness after the flood, they could hear the breeze blowing through the bushes, the crickets chirping in the meadow, and the birds singing in the treetops—if they listened closely enough.

Touching, tasting, hearing—that brings us to smelling and to Sammy Skunk, the forest gardener. Sammy loved all the plants in the forest. Most of all he loved the flowers and their beautiful fragrances. There was just one problem. Every time Sammy smelled a flower, someone else smelled Sammy!

"Hey, fella," Wally Weasel shouted to him one morning, "you stink!" The weasel hurried off, not stopping to think about anyone's feelings but his own. As I watched from my treetop, I saw a single teardrop run down Sammy's nose and fall to the ground.

I flew down to join him, trying to think of something to cheer him up. "Morning, Sammy," I said. "Those flowers are pretty, aren't they?"

He sniffed and nodded. "Sometimes I think flowers are the only friends I have. I wish I could keep them around all the time."

That got me thinking. "Sammy," I said, "let's meet at your house at three o'clock."

Sammy shrugged his shoulders. "Sure, Herman. Whatever you say."

At three o'clock I met Sammy on his front doorstep and handed him a large rolled paper. He unrolled it and read the words at the top:

Plan for Sammy Skunk's Greenhouse
Prepared by the firm of Owl, Robin, & Wren
H. Owl, Project Coordinator

His eyes opened wide. "A greenhouse . . . for me? It's . . . ." His eyes suddenly lost their sparkle. "I can't build it by myself, Herman. And how can I get help when no one will even come near me?"

"There'll be help," I answered.

Summer turned to autumn, and in the meadow behind
Sammy's house, a curious building began to take shape. At
first the only animals to see it were the builders: Sammy
Skunk, Rona Rabbit, Renaldo Raccoon, and Percy Q.
Porcupine. Gradually word spread. Before long everyone in
the forest had stopped by to take a look—from a safe
distance.

Autumn turned to winter. The structure, now finished, was covered with snow. Through the snowbank Sammy had dug a tunnel leading inside. It was through this tunnel he led all the forest animals for the grand opening of his new building.

"It was smart of you to hand out clothespins at the door, Sammy," honked Wally Weasel. "Otherwise nobody would have come."

Sammy showed them through the door and into the building's only room. "Welcome to my greenhouse," he said. There were gasps of astonishment—inside the building's glass walls were flowers of every description.

Chester Chipmunk gazed around the room, adjusting the clothespin on his nose. "They're beautiful!" he exclaimed. "Look at all the colors!"

"Oh, but there's more than just colors," said Sammy. "Take off the clothespin and you'll find out."

Chester did so and very carefully took a deep breath. "My goodness," he said, "the flowers smell even better than they look!"

The other animals took off their clothespins, too. Cries of delight filled the room as they recognized the scents of flowers they hadn't smelled in months.

"Well, if this doesn't beat all!" cackled Buford Badger. He turned to Sammy. "How'd you do it?"

"Herman Wise-Old-Owl drew up the plans. Rona Rabbit, Renaldo Raccoon, and Percy Q. Porcupine helped me build it," Sammy replied.

Percy spoke up. "We helped because we know how it feels to be alone. We wanted to make sure Sammy would always be surrounded by the things he loves most—flowers and their beautiful smells."

"But I didn't build the greenhouse just for myself," Sammy said. "I built it for all of you as a reminder and a promise. It's a reminder of all the smells covered by the snow, all the scents and fragrances of the summer. It's a promise that spring will be here soon."

"How do you know that?" asked Wally Weasel.

"I can smell it in the air," Sammy replied. "And so can you, if you try."

Spring did indeed come. From high in my treetop,
I saw the buds and blossoms. Then one day, as I was
watching the forest below, my glasses slipped from my
beak, fell to the ground, and shattered.

I went to Percy's office to see if he could fix them.
Along the way, I tripped and bumped my head, raising a
nasty lump over one eye.

"What happened to you?" Percy asked when I arrived.

"Dropped my glasses," I muttered. "Can't see a thing
without them."

Percy looked at them and shook his head. "It'll be a
week before your glasses can be repaired. Are you going to
be all right in the meantime?"

"Yes, I'll be fine," I said. "I won't leave my house for
the next seven days!" And with that, I staggered out of his
office.

The first day at home wasn't bad. By the second day I was bored. I was feeling sorry for myself when all at once I heard voices.

"Herman," said one of them, "it's me, Percy, and I've got Sammy, Rona, and Renaldo with me. We've come to bring you down out of your tree."

I felt the bump on my head. "No thanks. I already tried that, and it didn't work."

"Then try again," said Percy. "Come on, Herman, give me your hand."

"Well now, just . . . that is . . . what I'm trying to say is . . . Percy, I'm scared."

"Don't be," he replied gently. "Just think of us as your four other senses—touch, hearing, smell, and taste. We'll show you things your eyes could never see." He led me down the tree, and the five of us started off through the forest.

"Feel the ground beneath your feet?" Percy asked.

"Hm, yes, I do," I answered. "It was hard, and now it's getting soft and mushy."

"That's right," said Percy. "It means we're coming to a brook. Let's turn here and go another way."

Rona Rabbit spoke up. "Hear anything, Herman?"

"Yes . . . yes. Up ahead on the right, it's a buzzing sound, like . . . bees!" I replied.

"Good," she said. "That's using your ears! Come on, let's turn to the left."

Farther down the path, Sammy spoke up. "I smell something. Do you, Herman?"

I sniffed the air. "Why, yes. But I can't tell what it is. Can we go closer?"

"We certainly can," Sammy replied. "Just follow your nose."

I inched forward and bumped against a tree stump. "There's something on top of it," said Renaldo. "Why don't you reach out and taste it?"

I did and then said, "I'll bet I know what it is—your chestnut pie!"

"That's right," Renaldo said. "I remembered that you've never tried it, so I made one just for you. All of us decided it would taste better if you came to get it yourself."

I couldn't see my four friends, but I knew they were all smiling, and for the first time in two days, so was I! Now I could touch, hear, smell, and taste—and I had the whole forest to explore. But first, I wanted to eat a piece of chestnut pie!

"Here they are, Herman," said Percy. I felt him gently placing the new glasses on my beak. As he did, his smiling face came into view.

"Why, you look wonderful!" I said, turning around slowly. "Everything looks wonderful! Thank you, Percy. You've given me my sight back."